IN LOVING MEMORY OF MY
BELOVED BUNNY LOUIS

Our house became a home when Louis came
into our lives, the love that he gave us, really
opened up our eyes, the joy that he brought us
every single day, made our lives complete, so
special, in every single way.
Through hard times he brought happiness,
through sadness he brought smiles, for our
gentle giant companion was so loving and so
wise, his naughty side so innocent, his character
so magnificent so mischievous but so elegant, so
much passion in his eyes.

Then out of the blue the day came so early in his
life, struck down by an illness that took him
from our lives, our hearts are crushed, so broken,
both so empty deep inside, our beautiful boy
Louis taken before our eyes.
Our home is now just a house, now Louis is no
longer here, so empty, so cold inside, it's soul
has disappeared, for all of you who have never
known a love so bright and sunny, there is
nothing that compares to the love of our
beautiful giant bunny.
I miss you.

Lop Eared Louis

Chapter 1: Sunday morning

It was silly o'clock on a warm
spring Sunday morning when Louis
awoke, a big yawn, and a stretch, followed
by some breakfast, he was now ready for
the day ahead. He then noticed the time,
his humans are late, how very dare they!
They had not yet come downstairs to let
him out into the garden.

But luckily Louis is a house rabbit who
lives like a lord, so much so, that all of his
human friends call him 'Lord Louis.'

Lord Louis lives in the garage which is
attached to the house. His garage has been
made into bunny heaven, with toys,
tunnels and hides for him to explore. He
also has a large forage box and a huge
hutch where he eats and sleeps and uses
his litter tray.

His hutch also has 2 fleeces in there which keep him warm in the winter. The doors of his hutch are never closed, as his humans believe that all bunnies deserve freedom to roam in a safe place. They are not prisoners but members of your family.

Suddenly, Louis ears prick up, he hears footsteps, they become louder as they get closer and then.....silence, a short pause, before a long creak as the garage door is opened.

"Good morning Louis," says Kerry, one half of his adoptive humans, "...and how is my boy today?."

As usual Louis stops still, even stiller than a still thing that is permanently still! A guilty look on his face. "What have you done?" asks Kerry. Louis comes hopping over and begins to nudge Kerry's ankle, telling her off for being late downstairs. But he is a forgiving bunny, and will let her off for a nice head stroke, nose rub and a piece of banana, his most favourite treat.

Whilst Louis is happily munching away on his banana, Kerry wonders off to make a cuppa. She shouts upstairs to Paul, Louis other adoptive human.

"Do you want a cuppa making?"

"Yes please, oh and grab the biscuits, we can sit in the garden with Louis," Paul replies.

Louis hears this and comes happily hopping out of the garage, into the kitchen and then straight downstairs to the living room, where he sits patiently by the back door.

His ears prick up as he hears Paul's voice, followed by footsteps coming down the stairs. Paul is greeted by a very happy bunny, a bunny who cannot contain his excitement, hopping happily up to Paul, turns around and hops straight back to the door, a hint me thinks!

Paul follows Louis, unlocks and opens the door, with one almighty binky, Louis launches himself out into the garden. He runs around at an incredible speed, full of excitement, binkying to his heart's content.

Suddenly, Louis stops dead in his tracks, he stands as still as a statue, his nose sniffing the air. Rabbits use their noses to see who is around, they know who are their friends and who are not just by their smell. Louis sniffs the air one more time and then heads for the fence. He pokes his nose through the gap and is greeted by his friend, a guinea pig called Parsley.

"Good morning Louis," says Parsley.

"Good morning Parsley, I am sorry I am late, my humans were being lazy," says Louis. "My humans were late too, it must

be Sunday, humans are always late on a Sunday!" says Parsley. With that they both chuckled.

Chapter 2: Bartholomew

"Louis, what is the matter" says Kerry. Louis is as poised, ready to run. His nose is twitching extremely fast, sniffing the scents in the air. Suddenly, Parsley shouts from across the fence-

"Run for your life Louis, it is Bartholomew, the cat!" With that Louis runs and hides under the table where Kerry and Paul are sitting, dunking biscuits into their cups of coffee.

"Louis, you are a scaredy bunny, you are twice the size of Bartholomew, you should try and make friends with him" says Paul. Louis looks up at Paul and thumps in disgust at his humans suggestion, 'a rabbit being friends with cat, that is outrageous,' thinks Louis.

Parsley overheard Paul's suggestion and shouts over to Louis, "I think your human is mad, how could he suggest such a thing!

A rabbit and a cat becoming friends, this can never be, it will break all the laws of nature."

Louis now looks deep in thought, he shouts back to Parsley. "I am going to be the bunny that defied the laws of nature and make friends with Bartholomew. I will go down in history as the bravest bunny in the world....ever! The news will travel far and wide, reaching my distant relatives over on Watership Down. I will become a legend."

Parsley suggests to Louis that he should cut down on his sugary treats, they are not making him think straight, he's is becoming as mad as his human!"

Louis, now feeling brave creeps out from under the table, sniffs the air and shouts "Bartholomew, are you still there?"

"I am." says Bartholomew, "What do you want?"

Louis replies to Bartholomew with; "would you like to go down in history as the cat who defied the laws of nature, and be my friend?"

A long pause of silence follows, and then "you would be my friend? But that would defy the laws of nature...... Yes, oh yes Louis, I would love to. I have been hanging around hoping you would ask."

A nervous voice then shouts from beyond the fence, its Parsley.

 "Can I be your friend to Bartholomew?"

"Oh Parsley, of course, I would love to be your friend to" says Bartholomew.

"And you promise not to eat me?" Says Parsley,

"Oh Parsley, you are so silly, did you not realise that all the times I had been sat on your run, I wanted nothing more than to play? I was also guarding you," says Bartholomew.

"I do feel silly now Bartholomew, I thought you was waiting to eat me!" says Parsley.

All three of them burst out into laughter, and Louis shouts out "We are all going to be legends in the animal kingdom!"

Chapter 3: Louis and Bartholomew play "Catch a rabbit"

"Would you like to play a game Bartholomew" says Louis.

"Oh yes, what a wonderful idea, what shall we play?" says Bartholomew.

"Well," says Louis, "when my human, Paul, comes into my garage to take me out into the garden he sometimes chases me. I run through my tunnel, in my hutch, out my hutch, through my hide, over my bed and then I stop still. I lead Paul my human into a false sense of security.

"Sometimes I just give up and let him pick me up, sometimes I wait patiently, until he thinks he has caught me and then run out into the kitchen. He thinks we are playing a game, he calls it '*Catch a rabbit*'. I find it really amusing. I suppose it is a game, but a game I will always win."

"Oh Louis, that is so funny, your human sounds mad," says Bartholomew.

Parsley shouts from his run, across the fence. "My humans are too quick. They are as quick as a quick thing, and catch me every time, I have no chance!"

"Well," says Bartholomew, " I have no trouble going out, it's trying to get back in is the problem I have. I'm not sure who are my humans as I have many who look after me. I tap, tap, on their doors and meow as loud as I can, as I'm too short to ring the doorbell. Sometimes they don't hear me straight away and I have to sleep under a car."

"You can come and live with me," says Louis.

"You are so very kind Louis, but what will your humans say?" says Bartholomew.

"Don't worry Bartholomew, I will deal with them," replies Louis.

"Now Louis, shall we play catch a rabbit?" asks Bartholomew.

"Now you are talking," says Louis. "Parsley you are the referee, when we say now, you have to say, ready, steady, go and then count up to 30. If Bartholomew hasn't caught me by the time you have counted up to 30, I win!" says Louis.

"Okay," says Parsley.

"Bartholomew, are you ready? Louis, are you ready? Ready, steady, Gooooooo!" shouts Parsley.

Louis takes off like lightning! Binkying, turning, twisting and jumping, as he skillfully out manoeuvers his pursuer! Bartholomew is having trouble keeping up. Louis slips, Bartholomew pounces, but Louis recovers quickly and bolts off again.

The nearest of near misses, ever! Louis heads for the flower pots, he weaves around them, he stops behind one. Bartholomew sneaks up behind Louis, but Louis spots him, he draws Bartholomew in closer and closer then........he's off quicker than Usain Bolt!

"5,4,3,2,1, stoooooop," squeaks Parsley.

 Louis and Bartholomew both skid to a halt. "Louis wins, but it was close, there were a few hairy moments," squeaks Parsley.

"I'm not a *hare,* Parsley, I'm a rabbit,"
says Louis. With that all three of them roll

around the floor in laughter!

Chapter 4: Nap Time

"Louis, it's time to come in, it's nap time," says Paul.

Louis says "Goodbye Parsley, goodbye Bartholomew, I will be back later after my nap."

"Goodbye Louis, see you later," reply Bartholomew and Parsley.

With that, Louis hops inside, up the stairs to his rabbit cave. As per usual his hutch has been cleaned. There is lots of fresh hay inside, some Kale, dried grass and his favourite teddy 'Spotty Dog'. Louis loves to cuddle up to Spotty Dog when having a nap, he keeps him warm.

Louis has some lunch, snuggles up to spotty dog and falls fast asleep.

A few hours have past and it is now nearly early afternoon, Louis wakes up, stretches and has a gigantic yawn. He gives spotty dog a nudge and then wonders off to his forage box to see what treats he can find. His nose and front paws disappear inside the forage box. Sniffing away, looking for them tasty treats. Bingo, a piece of dried banana, his favourite. Next up dried Papaya, yummy!

'That foraging took too much energy, time for another nap. I think my bunny house looks extremely comfortable, I will sleep there,' thinks Louis. With an expert bunny flop on to his side, he falls straight back to sleep.

Louis must be the most spoilt bunny in the universe, he even has his own fridge! Filled to bursting with the finest vegetables that money can buy! Rabbits are very fussy, so only the best will do for Louis!

Kerry and Paul are ever so proud of him, so much so they tell everyone they meet about their very special boy. Louis means the world to them. Everyone who has met him, walks away smiling, gobsmacked on how clever and funny he is.

People have said that he is more like a dog. Louis on the other hand disagrees.

"I'm just like any other bunny. The difference is, I have been treated right; I have been allowed to thrive." And you know what, he is right. I could not of said it better myself. He brings so much love our lives and the world, for a bunnies love is forever.

Whilst Louis has his nap time, Kerry and Paul head off out to the farm shop to buy Louis his fruit and vegetables. As they walk into the shop they are greeted by Jo.

"Hello Kerry, hello Paul, how are you both? And how is Louis?"

"We are both very well," says Kerry.

" Louis is very well too, he's having a snooze at the moment" says Paul. "How are you Jo?" asks Paul.

"I am not too bad. I could do with a holiday," says Jo.

"Couldn't we all," says Kerry.

Louis basket is now filled up with kale, spring greens, Cavelo Nero, sugar snaps, cabbage, a small amount of carrot, but loads of carrot tops and of course apples and bananas. A fine feast for any bunny! They head for the till, pay for their shopping and say their farewells.

After leaving the farm shop, Kerry and Paul head off to the pet shop. This is where they buy Louis his favourite hay and maybe even a new toy.

Now, bunnies are curious creatures and know if something is not right. Sometimes they like it, sometimes they don't. If they don't like it, they will show their disgust by throwing a right tantrum. Louis used do this. It was hilarious when he threw a tantrum. He evicted everything from his hutch, including his food! There would be banging and crashing and thumping.

I dread to think what the neighbours thought!

Chapter 5: Brian the Wise

Tick tock tick tock tick tock dongggggg!

The clock strikes 6pm. Louis is laid on the kitchen floor guarding the fridge. For this is his human's fridge; it contains some of the finest vegetables - vegetables fit for a Rabbit or a Lord or Lord Louis!

He is not a silly rabbit, for he knows that if he lays in this awkward spot for long enough, his humans will give in and reward his stubborn patience. It might be with a piece of kale or a whole spring green leaf!

Result! stubbornness plus patience equals a bowl of chopped kale! Extremely yummy and now in *this* bunnies tummy.

Happy with his reward Louis heads off down the stairs to garden. He hops over to the fence and looks through.

"Parsley are you there?" asks Louis.......silence, he asks again....still no answer. With that Louis heads over to the other fence, he pokes his nose through and sniffs, in the hope that Aunty Marilyn is out in the garden.

'Hmmmmm, where is everybody?' thinks Louis. He then heads off down to the garden gate and lays down.

Suddenly Louis ears lift up, he's sniffing the air, frozen, as still as can be. In the distance, a noise. It is coming from the far end of the path, which runs along behind the garden. It is the sound of the patter of paws. This patter gets closer and closer and closer. Louis jumps up, he's poised ready to run. It is not a familiar scent, he is cautious; unsure. Who or what will walk along the path and past the garden gate?

The patter gets louder as it gets closer and then….stops.

"Who goes there?" says an old voice from beyond the gate.

"It is Louis, the gigantic fearless rabbit and Lord of House and Garden. Who are you?" says a nervous Louis.

A pause is followed by a deep laugh.

"Hah hah hah, ho ho ho, Lord Louis the gigantic fearless rabbit, I am Brian the Wise, King of Badgers from Dairy Crest Gardens."

"Nice to meet you King Brian" says Louis.

"And it is good to meet you Lord Louis," replies Brian.

"I must say, Lord Louis, you are a brave rabbit. All the other ones run away from us badgers," says Brian.

"You must know of my reputation for being the rabbit who defied the laws of nature and made friends with Bartholomew the cat?" says Louis.

"Nope, but I have now, Louis. You are now also the rabbit who has impressed and made friends with a badger. But not any old badger, the wisest of them all and the King of Dairy Crest Gardens!"

This was the start of a friendship that would last a lifetime and beyond; a friendship that yet again has defied the laws of nature!

If only us humans could learn from Louis, Parsley, Bartholomew and Brian.

Then and only then could they also defy the laws of nature.

Chapter 6- The Breakout.

"Louis, are you there?"calls Bartholomew.

"Yes I'm here," mumbles Louis, trying to speak with a mouthful of his humans prize geraniums!

"Oh good," says Bartholomew.

He jumps over the fence to see his friend. "I have an idea Louis, a cunning plan," whispers Bartholomew.

"Why are you whispering?" says Louis.

"I don't know," says Bartholomew.

"So, what is your cunning plan Bartholomew?" asks Louis.

"Well Louis, tonight we are going to free Parsley from his cage, we are going to break him out."

"Oooooooh, that sounds like fun, it will be like the greatest escape.....ever, count me in," says Louis.

"I knew I could rely on you," says Bartholomew.

The pair huddle up close, as Bartholomew explains his cunning plan to Louis.

"That is brilliant," says Louis.

"It is, isn't it?" says Bartholomew.

"It is the most cunning of the cunningest of cunning plans," says Louis.

The light begins to fade, giving the cunning two the cover they need to begin Bartholomew's 'most cunning of the cunningest of cunning plans....ever.'

Bartholomew jumps over the fence and sneaks up to Parsleys hutch.

"Parsley.......Parsley are you in there?" whispers Bartholomew.

"I am," squeaks Parsley.

Meanwhile, Louis is digging his way under the fence. His expert tunneling skills will be used to dig their way to freedom! This most cunning of the cunningest of cunning plans is fool proof!

Louis has made it under, he hops over to Bartholomew, who is hiding down the side of Parsleys hutch.

Bartholomew signals to Louis, then jumps onto the roof of Parsleys hutch. Louis is keeping a look out. He reaches over and unlocks the top bolt, success.

Bartholomew calls quietly down - "Louis, you're up."

With that he springs into action.

Standing up on his hind legs, he just about reaches the bottom catch. It creaks as Louis slides it open. He then bites the corner of the hutch door and pulls. A huge creek and........it's open!

Parsley you're free! The most cunning of the cunningest of cunning plans has........?

Chapter 7- They came, they saw, they ran away!

"What do you think you are doing!?!" shouts one of Parsleys humans.

This human is not to be messed with. He was once a prison officer; ironic really.

"Run for your life!" shouts Louis.

With that Bartholomew clears the fence with a single leap, out into Dairy Crest Gardens.

Louis runs back through his tunnel, into his garden. He then calmly hops into his living room like nothing has happened and lies down. He gives it a few minutes until the coast is clear, then hops back out into the garden.

He looks through the fence into Parsleys garden. Parsley is looking out of his hutch. His tiny feet gripping onto the mesh.

Louis calls out, "Parsley are you okay?"

"I am okay Louis, thank you for trying to break me out, oh and thank Bartholomew too. After all it was his plan."

A few moments pass before a voice from Dairy Crest Gardens calls out. It is Bartholomew.

"I'm sorry Parsley, my most cunning of the cunningest of cunning plans failed, your human is very clever."

"Don't be sorry Bartholomew, at least you tried," says Parsley.

"Aha, I have got it," shouts Louis. "It is the plan to end all planned plans! Even more cunning than the most cunning of cunningest cunning plans, even greater than the grr-"

Louis was rudely interrupted by Parsley and Bartholomew.

"Just spit it out Louis."

"Well, why don't we wait until the morning when Parsley is put in his run for the day. We then wait until his humans go to work. When the coast is clear, I can tunnel into his run and free him," says Louis.

"That is brilliant!" say Parsley and Bartholomew.

"It truly is the plan to end all planned plans," says Parsley.

Another day breaks, Louis is in the garden with his humans. He is biding his time, waiting patiently until he can unleash his plan. Time is ticking away and after what seems forever, Parsleys humans emerge from their home. They make their way over to his hutch, open it, pick up Parsley and place him in his run.

'Perfect,' thinks Louis, 'it is nearly time to break Parsley out.'

He hops over to the fence and lays down as if he is going to sun bath. Parsley's humans clean out his hutch and then head back into the house.

It is now time to tunnel Parsley out!

Bartholomew has turned up with precision timing, he stands guard. Louis begins to tunnel.

"Stop Louis, Stop," shouts Bartholomew.

Louis stops immediately. That was too close for comfort. One of Parsleys humans has come back out to hang the washing on the line.

Washing hung out, human has gone back in, coast is now clear.

Louis tunnels like super rabbit; within minutes he's through.

Oops, Louis calculations were off, his tunnel has come out on the far side of the run. But Louis thinks quick and acts fast.

He latches on to the corner of the run with his powerful jaws. Dragging Parsleys run across the garden and over the entrance to his tunnel.

Louis rises up like a Meerkat and looks around. The coast is still clear.

"Quick, Parsley, run," shouts Louis.

Parsley runs as fast as he can through the tunnel. Louis hops around to the opposite side of the run. Again he latches onto to the corner, again he drags it back across the grass. He then dives into his tunnel and

hops through. Mission accomplished,
Parsley is free, we have done it!

What shall we do now then?

I would like to say a huge THANK YOU to Jules Marriner of julesmarrinerbooks.com for her advice and of course her illustrations. Check out her website, Facebook, Instagram and Youtube pages.

I would also like to say a huge thank you to Parsley the Guinea Pig, Bartholomew the Cat and the Badger Brian the Wise. And not forgetting my beautiful boy Louis.

All the animals in this book were based on real life animals.
All the humans in this book were based on real life humans.

Will there be a sequel? Who knows. But have you ever wondered what really is beyond the garden fence?

I would like to give a special thank you to my Fiancee Kerry (Louis human Mum) for all the happy memories; memories that will never fade away.

Happy hopping and nose rubs,

Paul

Printed in Poland
by Amazon Fulfillment
Poland Sp. z o.o., Wrocław

63747186R00023